Light reading

F
LIGH

Race Ace Roger

written and illustrated by John Light

J.1060 46
Prep

Published by Child's Play (International) Limited
Swindon, England   **New York**
© 1990 M. Twinn   ISBN 0-85953-501-0   Printed in Singapore

Roger is an ace driver.
Mum is his usual engine.

She is very good in traffic.

Sometimes, Dad takes over.

He is a more powerful motor . . .

with more speed . . .

. . . but harder to control.

Dad is good over rough ground . . .

and he is amphibious . . .

Driving Dad is tiring work . . .

Roger is loved by his fans.
"What a dear little boy!"

Once, when Roger was looking after
his big sister, Katherine . . .

. . . they had an accident.

In Winter, a sleigh is best.

But the going is difficult in snow . . .

Sometimes, Roger drives a delivery truck.

There are some shocking drivers
in the supermarket.

When Mark was small, he drove a different model.

By the time Roger needed it,
Mark had converted it into a hot rod.

It was very fast,
but not good over rough ground . . .

So he rebuilt it to take passengers.

And he found a new engine . . .

Katherine is sluggish uphill . . .

But she is sensational downhill . . .